AGAVE BLOOMS JUST ONCE

JUST ONCE

(a-gah-vay)

HARBINGER HOUSE, INC.
Tucson, Arizona

Second printing 1992
Text copyright © 1989 by Gisela Jernigan.
Illustrations copyright © 1989 by E. Wesley Jernigan.
Alphabet "Santan" copyright © 1989 by E. Wesley Jernigan.
All rights reserved, including the right to reproduce this book, or any part thereof, in any form.

Library of Congress Cataloging in Publication Data
Jernigan, Gisela, 1948–
Agave blooms just once / by Gisela Jernigan;
illustrated by E. Wesley Jernigan.
p.   cm.
Summary: Illustrated verses present plants and animals of the desert from A to Z.
ISBN 0-943173-46-9: $12.95.
ISBN 0-943173-44-2 (pbk.): $7.95
1. Natural history—Southwestern States—Juvenile poetry.   2. Children's poetry.
American.   3. Alphabet rhymes.   [1. Desert plants—Poetry.   2. Desert animals—
Poetry.   3. American poetry.   4. Alphabet.]   I. Jernigan, E. W., ill.   II. Title.
PS3560.E7A73   1989   811'.54—dc20   89-35428
Printed in the United States of America

AGAVE BLOOMS JUST ONCE

(a-gaʹh-vay)

by Gisela Jernigan

illustrated by E. Wesley Jernigan

Harbinger House

Tucson

A is for agave
  it blooms just once, then dies.
B is for bobcat
  with sharp and searching eyes.

C is for coyote
　　howling wildly at the moon.
D is for desert willow
　　blooming fragrantly in June.

E is for tiny elf owl
   our smallest bird of prey.
F is for Fremont cottonwood
   giving shelter through the day.

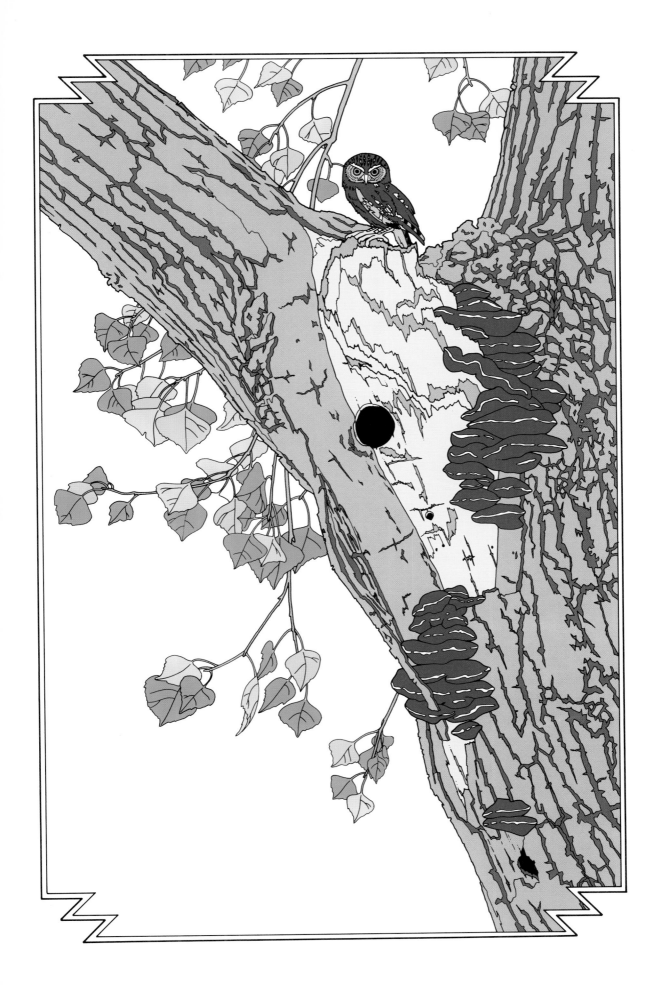

G is for Gambel's quail.
She nests along the ground.
H is for hedgehog cactus.
Its clumps are plump and round.

I is for ironwood
   Sonora's heaviest tree.
J is for jackrabbit
   loping by it swift and free.

K is for kingsnake
   striped in glossy black and white.
L is for limberbush.
   Its leaves are green and bright.

M is for mountain lion
  roaming through the rocky pass.
N is for nolina
  a flowering bear grass.

O is for oriole
  with feathers golden yellow.
P is for prickly pear
  bearing fruit both ripe and mellow.

Q is for queen-of-the-night
    blooming sweetly in the dark.
R is for ringtail cat.
    His tail a living question mark.

S is for sidewinder
gliding sideways through the sand.
T is for tumbleweed
tossed by wind across the land.

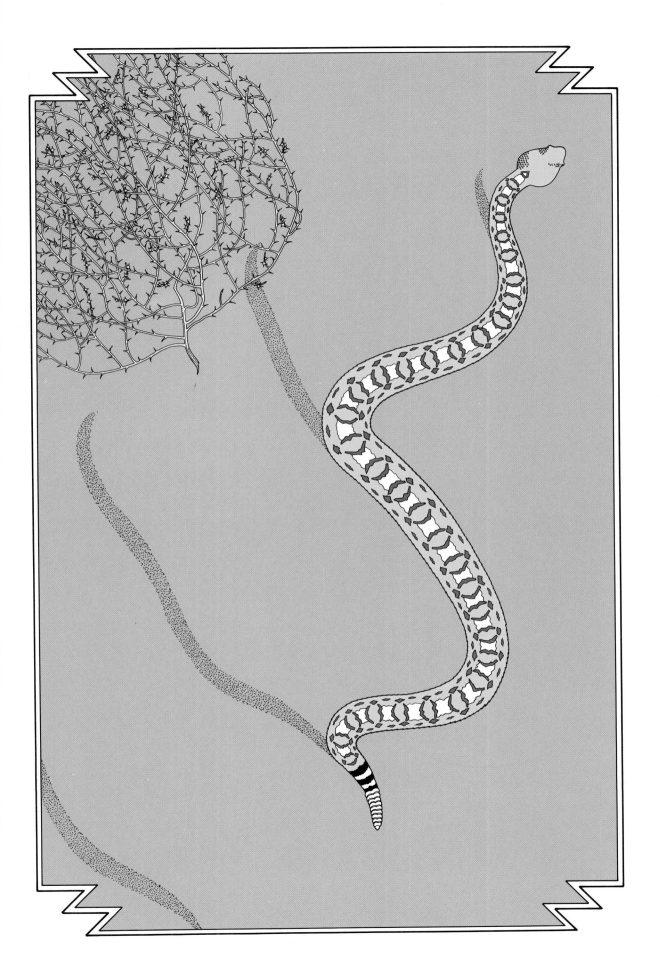

U is for unicorn plant.
Native peoples eat its seeds.
V is for velvet ant.
Nectar satisfies its needs.

W is for white-winged dove.
She coos a soothing chant.
X is for xerophyte
a desert-loving plant.

Y is for soaptree yucca.
  Soap is made from its roots.
Z is for zebra-tailed lizard
  gulping insects and flower shoots.

GLOSSARY

Agave (a-gah-vay).   Also called Century Plant, agave lives for many years before blooming, and is used by native peoples for food, drink, medicines, soap, and fibers.

Bobcat.   This stubby-tailed feline is the most common wildcat in North America.

Coyote (ky-ó-tee).   A fast-running wild dog which is famous for its series of barks and yelps, followed by a long howl.

Desert Willow.   Not a true willow, it has large, tubular flowers instead of catkins, and very long bean-like fruit.

Elf Owl.   A nocturnal sparrow-sized owl that eats large insects.

Fremont Cottonwood.   A streamside habitat allows it to be one of the largest native trees in the Sonoran Desert.

Gambel's Quail.   Both male and female have tear-drop shaped head plumes and like desert thickets.

Hedgehog Cactus.   It has a cylindrical shape and tends to grow in large clusters.

Ironwood.   A desert tree with purple blossoms and bean-like seeds. Its wood is very dense.

Jackrabbit.   Found throughout the American West, its long ears help keep it cool during hot weather.

Kingsnake.   A strong constrictor that eats birds, mice, and eggs, as well as other snakes, including rattlesnakes and coral snakes.

Limberbush.   Related to the poinsettia, this plant has colorful reddish bark, and bright, green, heart-shaped leaves.

Mountain Lion.   This solitary hunter used to live in many parts of the Americas, but is now confined mainly to mountainous, undisturbed areas.

Nolina (no-leé-na).   Related to yucca and agave, it has shiny, grass-like leaves, and tends to grow near oak and juniper trees.

Oriole.   Besides insects, these colorful songbirds also eat cactus fruits.

Prickly Pear.   Jointed cacti with flat pads and sweet, edible fruit.

Queen of the Night.   Also called Night Blooming Cereus, it has large, sweet-smelling flowers that only appear during a few nights of the year, usually in June.

Ring-tail Cat.   Not really a member of the cat family, this nocturnal hunter frequents rocky areas.

Sidewinder.   A rough-scaled rattler that uses "sidewinding" movements to travel quickly over shifting sands.

Tumbleweed.   Also called Russian Thistle, this plant is not really native to the Sonoran Desert, but is now our most common species of tumbleweed.

Unicorn Plant.   Often called Devil's Claw, it is used by native peoples for food and basket-making.

Velvet Ant.   A hairy wasp that scurries across the ground like a true ant.

White-winged Dove.   A desert dove that is especially fond of cactus fruit.

Xerophyte (zeé-ro-fite).   A term meaning "desert loving plant." Desert Marigolds are xerophytes that often grow along highways.

Yucca Elata (yuk-a ay-lot-a).   Also called Soaptree Yucca, these palm-like shrubs have one or more clusters of waxy, white flowers.

Zebra-tailed Lizard.   Swift-running lizards that often curl their tails over their backs to show off their zebra-like stripes.

All of the plants and animals in this book live in the Sonora Desert. Long ago this was the home of the Hohokam Indians, whose pottery designs are the inspiration for the stylized alphabet in this book. Except for the Tumbleweed (or Russian Thistle), all the plants and animals in the book are native to the Sonoran region.